DYING SCARLET

ALSO BY TIM BOWLING:

Low Water Slack (Nightwood, 1995)

DYING
SCARLET

TIM BOWLING

NIGHTWOOD EDITIONS

Nightwood Editions
R.R.#5, S.26, C.13
Gibsons, BC V0N 1V0

Edited for the press by John Pass.
Cover design by Kim LaFave.
Front cover photograph © Art Wolfe.

Published with the assistance of the Canada Council, the Province
of British Columbia through the British Columbia Arts Council
and the Alberta Foundation for the Arts.

Canadian Cataloguing in Publication Data

Bowling, Tim, 1964–
  Dying scarlet

  Poems.
  ISBN 0-88971-164-X

  I. Title.
PS8553.O9044D94 1997   C811'.54   C97-910757-1
PR9199.3.B636D94 1997

For Theresa Shea

with my love and respect

CONTENTS

I

II

III

I

Response to a Dead Chief

> To us the ashes of our ancestors are sacred
> and their resting place is hallowed ground.
> You wander far from the graves of your ancestors
> and seemingly without regret.
>
> Chief Seattle, 1854

Somewhere in southern Ontario, perhaps
behind a small brick church with a dying congregation
and a collection plate scattered with nickels
still graced with the head of Edward VII,
the tombs of my maternal grandparents,
thick and unread as Latin Bibles, gather snow.
No one brushes the winter from their names.
There they lie, Maggie and Arthur, dead
these fifty years.

And high on a bluff above the Pacific,
in the Coast Salish town of Tsawwassen,
my unnamed brother keeps his crib
in the perfect silence of his birth.
That sound in the pines is not his cry,
but only my parents' lost weeping.
Such a sweet place to be anonymous.
Every shadow that crosses the earth
unaware of his bones
carries the perfume of cedar.

Now, the black petals of another cold night
descend from the stars,
the only custom offered to my family's rest.
And they are tired of waiting for us.

Seattle, I confess,
the small tombs in my fingernails
are rarely visited by my eyes, and what the geese
pencil with their wings on autumn moons

falls smeared in random letters of the rain.
Seattle, I'm like anyone, more than 2000 miles
and a beautiful bluff from loving the earth:
finding our dead is the first stroke home
(whether Shield or Prairie or Salted Coast);
the body is a paddle we grip with our bones.

Family Bible

for my grandmother, Margaret Stevens (1881–1945) and her children, the three living and the fifteen dead

My totem is black as the rains of Haida Gwaii; black
is my totem with tears of generations, a burnt block
of cedar sinewed with Latinate phrases and names
of dead infants tallied each year to poverty's pox
and polio; my totem is black and keeps a Christ
in its grain, His words, His blood, and His high cross;
black is my totem and the eyes that raised it, from
bedside tables to parlours of grief; my totem is black
and lurid with the ink of an illiterate hand, mother
to Toronto's graves, daughter to a dashed Irish dream;
black is my totem as the winter rains of Haida Gwaii.

Let the spiders nest in the rot of its wood,
in the pith of faith that sways in the wind,
under the garish streak of the mask of pain,
under the slash of light, that naked bulb
above the childbirth bed, cast on the three
sets of twins uncried at the slap, cast on
the multiple coughs in the crib, cast on
the woman whose body is rain, and rains
through her days, her months, and her years.
Let the crows light and caw, let them sound
out the storms of the steaming kettles
that filled her kitchen as she inked the pages
and hummed the hymns, let their black wings
wreath the rented door while the undertaker
takes her teenaged girl unprettied to her
piece of earth. Let my totem eat the storm,
black into the burnt block, rain into char;
let it suffer the names of the little children
in a night without stars, as she did, turning
tear-streaked again to her husband's warmth.

Then let the sun break red over Haida Gwaii.

Snooker

The cue chalked, then clack of break.
A man drinks a beer before the Great War,
and again after the Second; he leans back
to watch the players shoot, and smiles to hear
in the din around him my grandfather's voice:
"In this game, it's not what you make
but what you leave." I think of the years
when the trench rats had gnawed his poise
to the quick, when the enemy had attacked
so often his steady hand continually flicked
the ash from his French cigarettes even when
there was no ash, and I understand how his tricks
on the table returned to him a kind of choice,
a right to be in control among his fellow men,
instead of a will that wags behind a loyal bark
and almost bleeds to death in a muddy foxhole
in some foreign black, boots brimful of his life,
gushing out from where the sniper's shrapnel
lodged. But more, I think of the man drinking beer,
watching others bend to the green felt and shoot,
their cues puffing chalk as the red balls clack
and sink into the pockets. He was young and watched,
and then he was older and then, like my grandfather,
he was gone forever from pool hall and beer parlour,
lost as those genteel terms for the places where smoke
gathered and hung like a slower-working mustard gas.
There is something in the look beside the event
that mocks us as it praises us, says of the past
that we are coming to it sure as the red drop
in our veins and on our tables, and that we're meant
to take the cue in hand or drink until the clock
breaks over the bar and all the faces change
to veterans of other wars, other lives. This look
that saw my grandfather fall in a distant dark
saw him rack the balls in the frayed cloud of smoke

in Legions and hotels, saw him hack out his last
strapped to a hospital bed, the intravenous-drip
into his veins a comic bow to fate, and now sees
my bent figure over the keyboard where I clack
out a break of letters, "It's not what you make
but what you leave." This is what the stranger meant
when he watched my grandfather be and die.
The praise is in the leaving of the field to time.

Nocturne

In the city of my mother's birth
moonlight drips from the bony flanks
of the rag-and-bone man's sorry nag.
A little girl in threadbare clothes
with eyes in her face large as
the holes in her stockings stands
shivering in the pale sheen. If
she had an apple, she would raise
it like a flame to watch the sinewed
darkness snuff it out;
if she could turn herself to grass,
she'd lie before the chipped hooves
and wait to disappear.

In the city of my father's birth
moonlight topples in Doric columns
from the starless sky, while a cold
wind paws the rack of used coats
stretched along a breadline. Blocks
away, wandering the ruins, a young man
pauses at the hissing entrance to a
blacksmith's shop. Snowflakes sink
into his skin like fossils, each one
moving closer to the molten core. If
he owned a horse, he'd shoe it with
fire so it would never slow down;
if he could, he'd forge his own hands
to its hooves and clap vast meadows
out of every moment's lost desires.

In the city of my birth
moonlight tips soft and grey
off the wings of swooping gulls.
The vertebrae of a dinosaur hangs
from a black bow in the harbour.

I stand on the third floor of a
skyscraper's shadow, watching
seals crawl out of the Inlet
to die; they cover the bodies
of derelicts with a deeper darkness;
they leave salt trails like a scatter
of panhandled coins. If I had my mother's
eyes, I would look only on grass until
her heart had meadowed and fragranced
the seas of her every breath; if I had
my father's skin, I would excavate
his past with the kisses of a woman
whose mouth settles softer than any
moonlight. But I can't give them
sweeter streets than what they knew,
nor clean mine of pain to ease
their worry. I have their blood
only. And blood, ask any traveller,
is the loneliest city.

Open Season

In the first autumn frost of 1963, my brothers
coasted their punt to stillness in some marsh reeds
at the mouth of the Fraser River, and shot a pair
of rainbows from the sky. The mantelpiece of my parents'
home would display those stuffed greens and blues for years;
I'd later steal the glassy eyes to replace my aggies
lost at school. But that cold morning, I wasn't around
when those quick mallards fell, when my brothers woke
in the same sparse room and spoke together almost
gently of the coming kill. I wasn't born. No myth
but theirs will line this poem, and no deaths either:
they're so young they can't foresee the rift
that time will tear between them. Maybe I know
where they were the night the two most famous shots
of the year brought down an empire's arcing prince,
but they don't know. Last month? Last week? Maybe
they were shooting pool at Dutchie's parlour or drinking
beer in the parking lot outside the rink. Maybe they
had bagged a ring-necked beauty in the pumpkin fields
behind some barn, or hung a spring net at the cannery.
Hell, maybe they pressed their mouths against our mother's
swollen belly and told me secrets no one else could tell.
They don't remember anything about those days, and if
you can't remember how you loved your brother in the breaking
dawn, why would you care about the famous dead, or the fact
they died at all? My brothers were close as those two birds
that flew above the marsh; they're not close now. Myth-making
isn't in their blood, or mine, and it's not my business
to wonder where they stood the moment that their friendship died.
Maybe they whispered something to me. Maybe they said, "Little
brother, you'll only know us when we're changed. But we were once
another way." Maybe they just laughed and said "he packs a punch."
I don't know. I might as well still be sleeping in the womb
with rainbow bruises on my temples, while my brothers pass
their frozen blue into my nephews' eyes.

Early Autumn: A Still Life

The cock pheasant and the fallen apple
(a transparent) share the top step
of the grey paint-chipped back-porch.
Both have been cut from their sap,
the bird from sky and cattailed ditch,
the fruit from its high branch.
On the laundry-line a bedsheet flaps
a rhythm quiet as a dying rain.
Against the side of the house
my brothers' mud-splotched boots
beside their shotguns catch
the final auburn of the sun.
There's a smatter of blood
along the snapped-tight beak
of the pheasant that's redder
than its red-brown feathers,
and a small bruise on the apple
where it struck the earth,
so that the former resembles
the moon with a single crater.
I am five and sitting on the bottom
of the porch. No one is looking for me.
It is the twilight time between supper
and my lukewarm bath. I know a few things
more than the things my eyes can see.
My brothers shot the cock with a gun
earlier that day in the potato fields.
It will decay as the transparent ripens,
one fall leeching the sap from the other.
And it will take a long time and no one
will even notice their traded skins.
And because I'm five and know some things
(and feel what I can't give a name to)
I have already sided with the apple.
I love how strange our changing happens.

The Death of Beauty

She was the last labrador of our childhood, and when
the grizzle finally frosted her black dance through
the world, she crawled one humid August afternoon
to the cropped grass under the pear tree and breathed
in rhythm to the buzz of the wasps and hornets
as active in the rotted, broken fruit as slaves over
blocks for the pyramids, until her shadow and herself
became butterflies mounted to the memory of earth.

We shared the gravedigging with the sun; it buried
her shadow, we buried her. Dad peered down the coal-shaft
of her body, sighing "poor old girl," while Mom waved
the flies away with a dishtowel. I heard strange voices
echo in the ground; they said "join us, it is warm here,"
and then the hornets' rasp of stone entombed all sound.
My sister wept seeds into the breathless soil.

The hole we dug was black as her. It was like we joined
her body to her shadow. Mom said "she was an old dog,
she had a long life." So the bones of Beauty
splattered like white rain from my father's hands
and the wasps dragged the red barge of her heart
under the deeper Nile.

I was young. I didn't know the sun would burn
my sister's tears; I thought they would grow
like the stars at twilight. But they burned. And mine.
The voices cried "plant more!", and how were we
to understand the words were human?

That was years ago. But still
I remember thinking
if Beauty's dead and buried in the ground,
oh sweet summer,
what's that lovely panting in my shadow?

Glass

Pane #1

I learned to skate in a World War II airplane hangar on the out-
skirts of a salmon-killing town. Converted to a rink, the propel-
lor blades gave way to shooshing steel, dogfights to dainty
arabesques. Who remembered Grable's ankles crossed or Miller's
music going down in fog? Now teenaged lovers necked along the
boards with no sense of irony to Engelbert Humperdink crooning
"Please Release Me." That was the late sixties, that was peace, that
was six years old. My dashing brother and his friends, freshly
graduated, drank BC's own Ben's beer in stubby bottles with the
bright tartan label and hung wicker potpourri and bunny ears
from the rearview mirrors of their first cars, the vroom of those
built engines all the darkened runway knew of power then. My
brother worked the ice. A red-jacketed rink rat, he swooped from
crease to crease to tend the fallen and toss delinquents (no fights,
no "crack-the-whip," no funny cigarettes). He could send a spray
Niagara-high when stopping at top speed. Sometimes he had to
dry a child's tears or bandage fingers cut by blades. Sometimes
young girls faked falls to have his lashes fanning them. Saturday
nights were fast and just got faster. The hit parade and hormones
whirled the crowd between the boards. I was lost in all that blur,
pushing a skinny iron cart, my ankles sliding on the ice. The
music was loud, the bodies hurtled by. When they held the Sadie
Hawkins skate, my brother sat me in the penalty box and gave me
chocolate bars. I watched a hundred tiny moons spin in the black
rafters and spill over the ice. Elvis Presley sang or perhaps Tom
Jones, the yearning voice reaching crescendo over the still heads
of the unchosen lined along the boards. Couples holding hands
passed between the moons in silent, slow formations. I almost
always fell asleep. And when I woke, I saw the thousand stars of
winter shining through the backseat skylight of my brother's mus-
tang fastback as he drove me home. They did not move. We sped
along the Fraser's banks in nearly total darkness, curving, racing
my brother's pulse-rate into town. And the stars did not move. I

lay on my back, half-asleep, peering through the thin glass. Sometimes I reached out to touch it, as though I could smear those still lights, my small hand, blood-fuelled, revving in the flak.

Pane #2

We had no spotlight on our cannery rental boat. Late August, the tide rushing out, and a chill in the thickening fog. We had drifted so far downriver, we had lost the channel home. I knelt in the bow to watch for driftwood and deadheads, to shout at each black shape. We idled slowly, our stern low with salmon, our engine barely audible above the current. My brother leaned his head outside the cabin window, straining, shouting "can you see the bank?" We had been awake all day and night. What we saw, we saw a second later. Cold tears ran from my eyes. I blinked, then blinked again. "I think there's something ..." but my brother didn't hear. Another second passed. There'd been nothing there. Once, I thought I heard him yell and turned to look. He'd pulled his head inside. I could just see his face through the fog and glass. A pale blur. A ghost behind the wheel. I turned back to the eastern sky. Every now and then, a star fell from a wisp of fog, like an earring appearing above a scarf, like an earring lying on the ice. Once my brother would have picked it up. Once I would have held it in my wonder. Now I gripped the anchor-cleat so tight the dried fish-blood cracked along my skin. Black ice of sky, black river. We crept towards the towhead and the hidden lights of town, two hung moons frozen on the running water.

Pane #3

Crossing Burrard Inlet in the rain with a female friend who is not a lover. How sad and beautiful the lights of the city are, neon streaks of red and green dripping down the windshield of the harbour ferry. It's nearly midnight on my wrist but always two a.m. Where are we going? Why can't we hear the engine that takes us to the other side? There are two dozen people here but no one is speaking. They all stare through the giant glass. My pretty friend looks like she would have been a girl to fake a fall on ice. A girl who would have waited for her song to choose a blood-warmed hand. Not one of mine. Mine have become the cold stars of my reaching and my fear. They do not move. I wish on them for all downed pilots, aging brothers, distant years. Now the only moon hangs swollen over the towns where we lived. How long can its clear glass hold? Red star, green star, the past that's flowing. We skate for all familiar light, innocent of the breakage in our stride, but of the breakage, knowing.

Money: A Confession

The men of my family never spend their change.
Weighted pockets, jingling postures, the fear
of public counting: these are my small legacy.
I'd sooner break a paper Queen than dole her out
in petty coin. The largesse of pride and insecurity;
bills from thin billfolds, a show for every waitress.
The world scorns a round man, and defines him by his edges.
My father's bedside table groans beneath its salver;
the bluenose and the beaver clink on that strange water.
"In wartime," my mother says, "he'd have drowned on leave
in a Yonge Street puddle before he'd empty his pockets.
A nice fate for a handsome sailor. That's your dad,
just like your brother, last of the big-time spenders."
I shared a room with my older brother and his mint,
our hardwood floor so iced with dimes I thought
the moonlight through our window froze in circles.
He'd come in at two a.m. and crash his pants
between our beds; that struck gong soundtracked
my dreams. But money's never been a family friend.
I have a little now, a pretty-sided salmon for
my mother's rainy day, a jingle for my nervous
hands, and a folded pretense for a pretty face.
But it won't stay. Already the coins have spilled
onto the table beside my bed, and across the floor:
I stand in the moonlight shedding nickels and dimes,
another tree in the unblossoming orchard of my line.

Half-Time at a Nephew's Soccer Game

The ghost of Degas must be here
sketching over his jockeys and dancers
attracted by the languorous grace
of these silent teenaged figures
standing in September sunlight
heads down, out of breath, sucking
the juice from sections of orange
stuck in their mouths like clownish grins,
a dozen boys in bright red shirts
sweating the last warmth of summer
into the lime-bordered grass.

A hand so in love with casual form
must hold them now, no different
than ballerinas at the training-bar
or jockeys in the stable,
the same unpractised pause
between the body's skill and truth,
the postures we acquire
and the human stance we can't unlearn.

An eye so enamoured with the speech of bones
must also see their lives unfold beyond
these years, the orange peels bleeding
in their hands, the spread lime
hot against their flesh
(soiled slippers and a broken saddle,
common accoutrements of such betrayal).

But still the painter's ghost
would sketch them on the field
to preserve their lines of perfect ease,
muscles loose before the whistle,
faces empty of desire,
as evening peels the citrus sun
and long, sure strokes of shadow
frame the softly stirring grass.

Swallow

Knife and thrower
the sharp edge and sharper aim.
And twilight a mask over
the blue face of summer.
That was when you came
to feast on termites rising
from the tall grass beside
our neighbours' rotting barn.
So many moving targets
that your flying could not
pierce them all. My parents
and I watched from their porch
as you failed to stop the twilight
of my last summer at home
from growing deeper and deeper
and finally turning into night.
When your act was over and you'd gone,
we lingered in that dark an hour or two
not talking much, until the stars
rose out of the earth.
We never thought to stop them
or the dawn. We'd have failed
of course, but then, some human love
is also knife and thrower, effect and aim
in one. Where did you go as we breathed
that final summer down? I'd like to say
you rested near enough to watch us also
lose the game, that you saw the hours
overcome our skill. But I can't say that.
Swallow, we tried, that's all I know.

In Edmonton, Thinking of My Brother

A new city, a new river,
but the blood in the world
is the same. Bruce, this
beautiful terror made me
dream your pure young coast,
the wheelwatch down from Rupert
and the waking shock that orca
gave your nodding bones.

Yesterday, in the valley trails
of the North Saskatchewan, I half-
dozed at a picnic table, head hung
over a book, the shouts of playing
children droning me to sleep.
What made me look? Some pulled
trigger in my blood perhaps? Our
father's eyes we share? I looked,
and the big buck tore across my sight
so fast he hoofed a red print in my chest.
Muscles straining, eyes crazed, he bounded
left, then right, then crashed again into
the trees. My heart kicked twice, as though
to help him run. What breath I had could not
slow down; it beat the air like hooves.

And then I thought of you, half-asleep
at twenty-one, wheelwatch for a seiner
running fast at night. Dozing, dozing,
when the orca clapped its black wave
at the bow. Beautiful terror! You felt
your blood uncoil like rope. Your
eyes could not stretch wider.

Brother, we are bound by more than memory;
something gifts us this mad joy.
Never mind the city or the river:
family is any star we choose; we
don't steer our lives by chance,
we steer by who we are and what we share.

To Vancouver, with Love

Odd, my inland stance away from you, each tremble
on the Richter Scale only a memory of a feeling
like birth-pangs in a woman's shadow still lying
on the grass beneath the apple tree since the morning
she cried out and was quickly driven to Grace Hospital.
Or is Grace closed? No? Then it must soon be closing:
who can afford Grace when a city might well be sinking
into the ground at any time, its postcard mountains all
consumed with fire? Painful to think of the scorched gulls
dropping in English Bay, I know, it's never easy losing
what we love, it's only human, and life is in fact beautiful,
just picture the deepening flush of spartans on the bough
or the delightful abacus of raindrops down a bedroom window
when another storm (the third this week) is registering
6.5 on the Melancholy Scale. But it's fine for me to sing
of the lush coast, being native-born, and gone, and so
ready in my nostalgic way to describe prairie lightning
as "long kelp on a black beach" to patient Albertans who
mostly think of the earth being torn apart as drilling
activity done for oil and wealth. Yet Grace is closed
here too, or something like it; the world is disappearing
underneath us all the time, and more than just hospitals:
look, the lava the salmon carry to melt the shore is going
sure as the moment it takes to add the rain up on the sill
is going and your own heart's life, so near to you and quaking
all the time with tremors and waves and fire, is quickly going.
What have you stored up for yourself in the closet, a little
cache of water and canned food? Nothing else? That's all?
But I am among the wild roses blooming and the derricks pumping,
and the shadow my mother left under the apple tree in 1964
is a cold slick and worth little to you, I know. Still, I'm storing
it away for when I need it, with the Fraser River and North Shore
Mountains, in case of emergency, in case of every day, living
as I do, as we all do, on unsure and lovely earth, picking
cool fire from the heavy branch, with or without the succour

of Grace or her sister, Compassion, their stone faces breaking under the force of our Scale. Vancouver, my vain city, you're not so unique; beauty teaches us terror the second we're born.

Sunday Morning

Snowmuffled churchbells wake me in the pre-dawn dark.
I have never heard them before, my whole life sleeping.
Why should I hear them now, low leaven for another day
just like my thirty years of days? Theirs is not the tolling
I was born to know, under fog and over tide, the calling
of the salmon home. Theirs is not a summons rung by rain.
But something in each muted sound, the distances between,
is ancient, how the heart must hear the human voice,
its bass-line prayer for time, more time.

Strange, to stir before the faithful of a city, half-
asleep and breathing to a half-familiar, distant knell.
Slowly, as the dawnlight gutters in, so frail a whisper
could well snuff the future out, I see the rotted whale
again, its mass of black scarred white from scraping stone.
A baby nar, some adult says, closing his lips
around a steaming mug beside the driftwood fire.
I stand within the circle of the light and stare.
The ocean falls, and pauses, and falls. A wordless speech.
I know the belly of the whale burns red as flame and
that a sinner sleeps within. Will he walk out and join
our bodies gathered on the beach? Or will he choose
another living in the fire? I watch until the surf
and lateness draw my senses in.

How long it takes our lives to step into their changes.
I'm waking now to muffled heartbeats dying in a body far at sea,
a body rolling like a black pew torn from an island church.
Faith is the belly and fire that keeps us, the silence
between each breath and word, and how we know to live there.
When I rise and look out the window on the reddening city
not my own, the bells will toll softer through the heavy snow.
I won't go with them where they're leading. Circle and creek
becoming one. The sweet salt, memory, calls me home.

II

Greeting the New Year in Vancouver

Four a.m. I step outside
and the tinsel grass crunches:
a few feet away
on the neighbours' huge Victorian house
icicles rare as mammoths' tusks
glint in the year's first starlight;
someone's still awake, a fire
veins the beast's chilled gaze;
he stirs, snorts great grey breaths
in the pre-dawn air, shakes
a little snow from his burning hide
but refuses to lumber off.

Hunger without direction defines the hour.
I can't sleep for dreaming. The new earth,
palely lit by past millennia,
retracts its ladders; no one walks here.
Poseidon, blue-lipped in the fishpond,
lusts sadly for his blue Aegean,
while the Japanese carp, stiff as coins,
float wishless in the ice.

Four a.m.
The planet turns slowly
like a man looking back
at his footsteps in the snow.

Once more I am resolved
to fresh divinities, brighter schools.

Great Blue Heron

Prehistory stands in the saltmarsh
on stem-thin legs sinewy
as a sailor's twisted hemp
and cries once, brief and hoarse,
the bugle blast of a tubercular angel
heralding another apocalypse

then lifts into the ashen sky
ponderously
and skims the tufted cattails
along the muddied riverbank,
large eyes still reflecting
an earth before time,
blinking away with jaded calm
armies heaped below China's Great Wall,
the first stigmata cooled on the cross,
the basketed pallor of French aristocracy,
all the race's casual carnage
running dark and constant beneath
the beating of awkward wings

now flies through a light drizzle,
an umbrella with a broken spine
swept against the darkening sky,
a failed sketch for Kitty Hawk
slowly erased from the page

and reappears at dawn
alone as always, perched on a rotted piling,
hunched in its shabby raincoat
like a terrorist, smoking long
cigarettes of mist,
cooly staring at life,
waiting for the final bomb to go off,
waiting for the end of history.

Snowy Owl After Midnight

I like to believe he waits for me
in the cottonwoods along the river,
eyes trained on the porchlight
of my house;
I like to believe his blood stirs
at my presence, in a way unknown
to him, but that he also understands
the heightened smell of joy and fear
my bones give off
as I shut the door behind me
and plunge into the stars.

It is so quiet at this hour,
just the two of us awake,
each hunting in his way
the small gifts of the night,
what he seeks in the long grass
and marshes, what I seek
in the unpeopled silence:
at first I thought I followed him
along the dyke and through the fields,
privy to a ritual strange and
wild in its solitude;
now I'm not so sure.

For miles
he wings above my shoulder
quick and small as those moons
we watched in childhood
from the backseats of our parents' cars,
those moons that always raced us home,
that we could never lose

and when I stop, he's there,
settling on a fence-post or piling,

diving behind a clump of trees;
never a shriek from the grass
never a word from my throat:
we have circled each other's silence
this way for months.

Again, tonight, I wonder
what he would tell me if he could;
would he say the blood that calls him
to the earth is a blood
he does not understand?
Under these drumming wings I wonder
what death does he expect
my clipped, pale hands to make?

I would say to him now,
this blank page riffling in the night,
this beating heart of a snowman
extant from some boyish dream,
brother, I have stopped my ears against
the blood that calls me to the earth
but I will move here with you
in its dark and silent flowing
as long as breath is given
and your vigil burns white fire in the trees.

Golfing at Beach Grove

for Curt Stadel

Just dawn. Ocean mist over the fairways,
and the sun somewhere behind it
like an eagle's heart, calm
but destined for a racing warmth
when the white burns off. We're smooth-
skinned at twelve and playing through
a foursome of old men we can barely see,
their voices rough and low as the grind
of tide on rock: "Sure, boys, go ahead."
And we stride past their blurred forms,
haying the yardage with our long irons,
sowing dew into the path ahead of us,
the green earth so wet we might be
sinking slowly into the advancing sea.
It's April. The rhododendron-tips
split open to the heaviness of colour
and the tall cedars sport corsages
of birdsong on their starched lapels.
We speak of lowest rounds and one-
putts and straight approaches with
soft landings, when we speak at all.
Mostly, we walk apart, keep a silence
whose substance now is as lost to me
as the mists and voices over that course
we played a hundred times before we turned
thirteen. Whatever we thought of, whatever
we said only to ourselves, or didn't say,
how the smell of the earth or the nearby sea
moved from our senses to our dreams, or
stopped somewhere along the way, is gone.
We sank or yipped the putts, we marked
the scorecards, and we broke the mist
with swings until we felt the talons
of a later hour at our skin.

My last time home, I drove out to the course
at night, along the ocean till I reached
the fairway of the par-four tenth
you once eagled from two-hundred yards.
I sent my headlights' arcing shots
between the cedars at the green
and in the silence strained to hear
them drop. I thought I could smell
the rhododendrons though their season
had not come; it was only my hand
on the wheel that showed the years
we'd lived and hadn't kept in touch.

I sat there for a while, the eighteen dark
pockets empty of all hands and waiting for other
boys to reach down until they find the moment
when they become the blurred pauses of old men.
So close to the sea and its familiar sounds,
even this landscaped earth could not deny its needs,
eighteen pried oyster shells longing for their loss,
a round white jewel to complete their purpose,
but now only winter moonlight and a light frost
rolled towards the cups. I stepped out of the car
and walked in the sure trajectory of its beams
and tried to breathe an April from the air,
asking, what do our hearts hide from in youth?
And the question went straight out in search of a sun
that hasn't burned through to us yet, but will,
flies out from our longing in search of a purpose,
and will find one, in this endless reaching for blossom,
along this green path that we'll always walk blind,
until the earth will have the very pearls of us.

Incident at the Towhead (Canoe Pass)

In the middle of the night
on a high tide running hard
from the mouth to the Gulf
I clambered half-asleep
from the cabin to the bow
to pull up the anchor

and I tripped and fell
sideways. I remember the sky
very black and constellations
like frosted twigs that snapped
as I reached out my hands
for balance. If I had plunged
forward I would certainly
be dead now, the tide so fast
and my brother not watching

but it was over in a second.
I hit the cabin-edge and caught
it with one hand and kept myself
from falling in the river, how
I managed it I don't know but
I did and my heart was pounding.
On the banks there was no sound
and the cabin lights of the other
boats at anchor were still dark.
I thought, how fast we move from
fact to memory, but my brother
put the boat in gear and I had
no time to mull the second over.

The way the body rights itself
in peril, does the spirit work
the same? On what bow do we slip
in terms of faith or love and with

what sure instinct adjust ourselves?
The darkness that flows by, the dark
that is over and around us, the silence
of the night, and the sudden recovery
of what we need to live, the clutch
of an edge and the spirit
pounding though we don't feel it,
the self back in gear too quickly,
the earth turning its mossy bow
on the tide. Fleet ghost, pick up
your chain and go.

The Canola Fields Near Tsawwassen

To reach the ocean
we must cross the surface of the sun
shielding our eyes
like the nineteenth century
before a Van Gogh canvas,
we must part the rays, step
by step refract the light:
such a distance to the horizon
and it keeps curving away.

Our shadows cannot fall;
they're bottled ink inside us.
To one side, the hundred baking
ovens of a stalled coal train;
to the other, tomorrow.
But we don't seek that rising.
We only want the sad blue
tremble of home.

Such a long journey
even though
in this light
we soon become light

and the seagulls float behind us like our bones.

Stray Dog

Most true it is, that I have look'd on truth
Askance and strangely; but, by all above,
These blenches gave my heart another youth

—William Shakespeare, *Sonnet CX*

He befriended me or I befriended him. It's no clearer
now than it was in the days when such friendships were
fast-struck between our kind along the mouth of the Fraser,
quiet boy and cur, one's dreams and games, the other's
cockeyed walk and mangy fur, and the long going-down
of the sun in summer.

On the edge of the city, far from a home, I was caught
in the pelt and fray of a thunderstorm, and I sought
refuge in the only shelter in that bleak
landscape where the pollutants of industry
married the first blooms of a sick blackberry
bush cowering like a hobo in his rags by railroad
tracks headed to nowhere. An old phone booth, cracked
and receiver-less, but with a door whose hinges looked
to work. I made for it, desperate, as the sky drumrolled
my progress through the sudden dusk, and the air
became thick as fathoms round my chest. Suddenly,
off to one side of my haste, he was there,
like a shred of linen torn from a clothesline
and blown by the wind at knee-height until he
almost knocked me down. But I was glad for life
in that black place with the sound of the rain
and my ragged breath fighting for supremacy.
Besides, I was not so old I'd lost the memory
of running to his pace, or of those familiar eyes
that turned at nearly every chance to check
that I was real, a creature fearing cold who'd seek
relief. In truth, I was grateful for the company.

We reached our shelter as the lightning struck,
and cozied in to ride it out. Soon, the musky stink
of soaking fur became a challenge to my generosity,
and the damp press against my legs, and the fetid breath
of the trash he'd fed on, and the soured milk scum
of his left eye, worked against his stay. And from
the look of the horizon, it seemed the heaviest
part of the storm was still to come. I had reasons,
solid, selfish, human, but I couldn't put him out.

I tried to shut my senses down. From my coat pocket
I removed a book and started to read, first to myself,
and then aloud, almost frightened by this closeness
I had not known in twenty years, the odd intimacy
of being kin under the whip of elements, muscle
and bone and the need to survive. I couldn't see
the world anymore through the fogged-up glass,
and soon I couldn't even read the words. Still,
time passed. Darkness seeped through the booth
like muddy water through a sieve, but it was today
becoming yesterday not tomorrow, it was my mouth
chanting a child's rhyme I had never remembered,
and it was a chance to live a boy's hour
in a man's year, while the dog at my feet
stopped whimpering at the sky, grew quiet,
then quieter, then closed his eyes and slept.

When I finally pulled back the door, and came into the air
so fresh with rain-scent, the moon was shining in the west
and shimmering off the greasy road and the rusted rails,
scrubbing a winter's worth of travel from the hobo's clothes.
I thought briefly of the pain and tenderness of the rest
of my days, of this moment becoming tomorrow becoming the past
becoming everything we know about time. We were back in it,
the long begging for the butcher's bone, the hunger for the sun,
the crouched sweet darkness always parallel to sight.

Autumn

The axe-blade falls and splits
the cedar block. At the exact
second the wood opens, I hear
the cry of Canada geese rising
from the marsh, as though I'd
set their voices free, as though
their voices split the block.
The vibration in my arm is partly
echo, partly flight. Who am I
to stand between the seasons?
Over my shoulder, three leaves
on the maple tree decide to blush
a deeper red. And farther, higher,
smoke from a leaf-fire wraps around
a blue pillar of sky. I can't see
the geese, but their cry is louder.
Winter owes us nothing but its cold.
I throw the split block on the pile,
drop the axe. And stand, staring.
It's always this way:
the cry of geese is the smoke,
and our silence the fire.

One Morning, Early

The last spiderweb I broke
joined the fishnet fence around
my father's vegetable garden to
a ripening pear on the neighbours'
loaded tree. Six feet it spanned
at a sharp enough angle to need
twelve feet of web. But the central
design was small, and I walked through
the strand on the garden side
too late to catch myself. I wasn't
going anywhere important enough to
break a spider's heart. That day
I walked for the pure sake of feeling
August on my skin. Then I crossed
the line, a marathon tape for dragonflies,
and watched it scythe to a gentle stop
in the wet grass full of fallen pears.
And I noticed the other strand.
What does a spider know about time, to
trust its art to something doomed?
Or would the craft have been undone
under moonlight at a tremble from
the branch we cannot feel? If so,
I had not been bargained for, by
August or the world I'd ruined.
If not, I had fallen, and perhaps
am falling still. September, let me walk
with care through your gold, decaying rooms.
I am holding fast to the swollen light.
The spider trusts its art to something doomed.

Old Barns

Starlight especially seems to love them;
its fractured brilliance angles in
the broken loft
with so much ease and warmth
it's as though the long, gold needles
of a distant harvest
had fallen through the galaxies
in search of home, as though
somewhere in the immensity of darkness
a wagonload of hay had overturned
and centuries later settled in beside
the swallows' nests and spiderwebs
like a living thing that knows
where it belongs.

This is the power these structures have,
the sense of sanctuary they possess;
animals sheltered from the storm
men and women laying down their tools
children dreaming in the lofts ...
disparate lives and disparate refuge ...
so the wind plays through these gaps
like the collective heaving of a sigh
that the very walls accommodate
as if to say "we understand."

And driving by them, autumn nights,
splashing their planks
with the milk of headlight beams,
I have often felt an urge to turn inside
and watch the needles streaming down
in crossing lines of pure geometry,
the delicate puzzle of time and space
suddenly woven into an owl's flight

and swallowed by the air;
but I have rarely stopped:

somehow it seems enough to know
they still exist, these wooden caves
crowded with their ghosts of early dreams
and honest labour, gathering
the same slow crop of the stars
year after year, and promising
these few spilled wagons for us all;
a subtle interplay of gold, a little silence,
and the corner of a field to vanish in.

Pacific Sockeye, Moving East

Late October.
The spawner kicks across the border, crosses
below the Rockies, becomes the gushing wound
in the gold flesh of the shot doe, becomes, oh,
becomes the quick shock of fox that clings
like a blinked lash to the corner of my eye
when I walk out in the flakes of snow.
The world is waking to its purity again,
the flesh of the apple recomposing around
the crawling worm of sin. And then I catch
you in my gaze, blush of life, old scale,
soft fur, fruit-bloom—the scarlet strip
of possibility, the flesh of the apple
falling in love with the idea of a skin.

Dying Scarlet

> I have had a great deal of pleasant time with Rice lately,
> and am getting initiated into a little band—they call
> drinking deep dying scarlet.

—Keats to his brothers, January, 1818

John Keats and his circle in their cups
died scarlet. And the poet's life
to its dregs did the same, his linen
bedsheets and nightshirt finely spotted.
The world loves him for drinking so deep
from the few years he had, for those pretty
tipples he took from his days' good wine;
the world honours blood flushed in a pale
brow that leans over blank pages in candle-
flicker, giving joy, believing. Vitality
is beautiful even coughed on a lace cuff,
o little red cosmos, little red heaven,
that last breath exhaled before dust
and the cold grave smothered his youth.

I don't know anything certain about the dead
except they're gone, young Keats and his brothers,
the two women named Fanny he loved, his friends,
the publishers who respected his art, the guardian
who didn't, Shelley with a drowned volume in his
shirt-pocket under Italian stars, gone. A century
of letter-writing, gossip, tuberculosis and poems.
And I don't know where the spirit of any poet goes
if it doesn't die scarlet wherever it can, Keats's
joy in October sunsets over the Adams River, full in
the salmon's scales as they scrabble to spawn before
the air eats to nothing their lace-threaded bones,
Keats's fear in the eyes of the ring-necked pheasant
shot out of its heart in the blue skies of my marshland
home, the long script of its death trailing off

into the ditches and rushes. I have heard the music
of his lines gasped from a thousand slack jaws
while the world stood crowded on the riverbanks,
amazed; my hands have touched the spots of his truth
on a thousand downed wings still quivering in frost.
In my wrists live the ghosts of all the words
ever written in his, and his Queen's, English;
they gather in my pulses, drinking life, dying scarlet,
unrestrained in their gaiety and rowdiness, dying
like the salmon and the pheasant and the flushed
eves of fall, dying as a poet dies, face turned
towards what's left of his life, the spatter
of his joy's heaven on his clothes,
the light going out on his page forever, the wax
of the last candle on his nightstand melted down,
as he lies grieving for every second he's lost
of the sun: I don't expect to know the vivid dawn
that finally dissolved the gay circle of Keats,
but if I'm blessed to die scarlet on my native ground,
let the wind dig a grave for my pallid song.

Neepawa

If there are angels here, we cannot see them.
If the stone wings of someone's small eternity
strain for the prairies' shy starlight
—peeking like children from behind the dark skirts
of this brooding Manitoba storm—
they will reach whatever heaven they must reach
alone:
who cares for the dead, in the night, in the heat,
in a lonely coffee shop
in the June-dry middle of a world
most hearts rise from like startled pheasants,
alive, alive, but craving the wet ditch
and the sweet-rank whisper of origin?

I am thirty-two hours by bus
from the flowing black hair of seine-boats
shimmering with the blossom of salmon
and from my own bark angel sinking
his wings in the silt.

Somehow, the word "distance" hangs
from the cracked lower lip of the elderly woman
who takes my few coins; I can't bear
the blue moonlight she carries in her eyes.

"Do you remember a woman …?" I almost ask,
but who doesn't remember the tall blood
that presides over each lost cemetery,
the singing made stone
                    and risen?

Akhmatova

Searching for a good translation of a woman's heart,
the joy and pain that live across the sea, beneath
the ground, I find my body swaying to the only Russian
phrase I ever understood in the marrow not the mind;
"Shy boo! Shy boo!" the mufflered Moscow crowd shouted
through my parents' tiny black and white as the point-
men made their passes back and forth. "Shoot the puck!
Shoot the puck!" And all their muscles strained to hear
the heavy slap of wood on ice, as all my muscles feared
the flashing light behind our net. The only phrase, but
in it throbbed the longing of a common passion.

Now the typing script of forward passes lies on a page
long turned; I am not the boy who wears a leaf upon his
chest and chews his nails over finite games of skill
and chance; the crowd is no subsided cheer, but thousands
leaving for their lives, the heartbeats falling from
the branches, the moon out wandering in her muddied
wedding dress, crying the bloodsoaked phrases
of the only language pure enough to translate
our spirits into grass, the grass we pray
our children learn their swaying from.

Depression

for Norm Sacuta

The moon drops a sack of crushed grapes
from my shoulders. Another muggy night
and this is all I have for company,
musk at my pantlegs like a dog.
It's been a week of thunderstorms,
that frayed black rope in the sky
I dread to see the end of, the flashes
of photo-hounds at the hanging. Now
the moon is a letter on a black-oak desk
I haven't started to someone I love.
I'm a happy man, most days, but white
limbs that vint a sweet wine from
the body's cast can leave a bitter
aftertaste. That is, a memory of love
can make us harsh on what we have.
Hear that? The hour brings the rope.
The musk puts its paws against my chest.
There's nothing for it, life IS Russian.
Tell Gogol my shoulders drag his overcoat.

Chinese Take-Away

Always seeming half-asleep
behind the counter
of his tiny establishment
when the bell over the door
tinkles my entrance,
the smiling, bald-headed owner
nods as usual, says
with exaggerated politeness
"one moment, please, one moment"
then vanishes through a narrow opening
to that mysterious pungent world
of woks and stir-fry steam
where shivering prawns try on
their skins of gold
and the chopping of the suey
proceeds in perfect silence:
always "one moment, please"
and the magician's skillful exit,
no doubt explained away
by routine, quaint habit, etc.

O, but patrons of the Golden Dragon,
alone in the mouth of forked flame,
snowflakes melting on your hair,
understand he's making special fortunes
just for us, typing them out
on a battered manual, the words inspired
by our body language, the look in our eyes,
as we stand there, hungry,
in his somnolent world,
not thinking of the future or the past;
understand there's an unspoken love
in the commerce of this food
and that all the tiny ribbons
we study later at our tables

in the dim light of the Evening Star
form a long white highway
of what humanity seems incapable
of saying to itself:
"my fortunate friend,
your days will be blessed"

and suddenly
the gift of warmth
is in our hands.

Having Lunch in a Tea-Room
Full of Elderly Women

The clink of spoons in china cups signals
the judiciary of the ampersand:
& so and so's daughter has a new job
& my grandson's marriage is troubled
& why shouldn't she spend a little of the money
now she's on her own?
& I don't know why the government insists on
& have you read that book, seen that show?
& the cheesecake's wonderful, but terribly rich
& when the moon lies on her back, the salmon
will surely run
& who ever mourns the forgotten miles
on all the tires in all the junkyards of the world?
& death is simply the moment when
the wind shears like sheep all the dandelions
drowsing in the midmorning sun.

I feel I should rise and approach the bench
I feel I should plead for leniency;
there are blades of grass in my skin
that ghosts have never used to whistle
their loved ones home.

When I leave
I push back my chair so softly
only the spoons in their fragile cups
sing out a silver mercy.

Sad, and Turning Pages
in the Oxford English Dictionary

1607 Shak Coriolanus IV i 30
I go alone Like to a lonely Dragon

No one was lonely before Shakespeare.
The feeling did not fall from tongue
to lip to air. Men stood in nights so
black they couldn't see their hands
and wept, saying nothing to the moon.
Women pushed suckling mouths from their
breasts, and gasped in mute despair. Such
a small key, such a sharp click in the
soft red lock. One mind made the turning,
and millions cried "Oh Christ, I'm lonely!"
One pen scratched the parchment, one hand
held the pen, one heart moved the hand:
"lonely" whispered in the silence, falling
from tongue to lip to air, a kiss for
lost hands, a kiss for sore breasts.

Shakespeare's been dead 400 years,
and we're lonely,
the moon knows the weight of our breath,
and we're lonely,
a million mouths form hunger
in the cradle,
and what else is our genius,
but this lust to speak full life,
the dream on the lip, the tremble?

Venus Time

> The period of rotation, 224 Earth days, is the slowest of
> all the planets and is longer than the period of the plan-
> et's revolution, so that Venus' day is about ten percent
> longer than its year.
>
> —From a science textbook

In your absence, everything is motionless.
My pain, not the sun or the earth,
is the centre of the universe.
Even astronomers of the sixteenth century,
Copernican irreverents holding quadrants
to their widening gaze, predicted
that your star would burst
and leave my planet cold: later,
Kepler with his eyes still sore
from telescopic staring at the sun
wrote in fiery letters
of a cataclysm due to fall,
and Galileo, dropping lead and feathers
from Pisa's Leaning Tower, knew
that all the heavens changed
only when one chose to see them change.

I haven't made that choice.

Ptolemaic to the bone, I still insist
your orbit is around me, in a space
so infinite and beautiful it contains
all knowledge and all truth;
I have burned every other life
for treason at the stake,
ground the strongest lenses
into dust for the solar winds
to scatter as they will:
my firmament, my faith, is fixed.

Yet here, now, among the few objects
you left behind, the cds and the books,
a lipstick burning on the bathroom vanity
red as Mars, all the nebulae of dissolution,
I know what it means to live on Venus time,
growing ancient by the hour, weak and frail,
pointing obsolete instruments at a just-discovered world.

One Year Later

A black fly the exact length of your phone number
settles on the back of my hand. I wasn't thinking of you.
Now the summer smears blackberry juice on my skin
and the smell is sweet. Now the little train of longing
pulls forward; the old dials tremble in my fingertips.
I will not think of you. My voice will never again leave
its message after your calm explanation of absence.
The fly is seven dark raindrops that drench my whole body.
The fly is seven dips of a quill in John Donne's midnight.
The fly is the scar your mascara left when you cried.
And the fly, like my longing, must rise again to its life.

Your Faithful & Obedient Servant

I would like to hear from you more often,
at least twice a day, as in the nineteenth century
when both the dawn & the twilight mailed
their mysteries in the guise of words,
every day that first gift of the sun & stars
sprinkled on each envelope
to massage my empty hands—ah—like a tray
of butter, a saucer of milk, slipped
into my life by someone sensitive to my need;
& I would like to open every letter slowly
with a beautiful paperknife that was my father's
& his father's before,
& I would like to stay late in bed
in my silk pyjamas & handlebar moustache,
nibbling a piece of toast, sipping a cup of tea,
reading every word with care, every graceful stroke
of the calligraphy you learned from the Mesdemoiselles
of your foreign schools,
& I would like to dream of the moistened nib
of your fabulous peacock-quill pen
sliding across the supple vellum
that was your mother's & her mother's before
that feels every bit as soft as
I remember your skin, so far away,
& when I come home in the evening, tired,
carrying a hundred years without you on my eyes,
when I leave the streetlamps & the fog behind,
the clop of muscled horses on the empty cobblestone,
I would like to find, on the mahogany table
in the hall, at the foot of the winding stairs,
as I sink slowly in the plush damask
of my high & lonely station,
a nest of your pale letters
glimmering in the first electric light,
the blood-red wax that seals each one

like a beauty mark I have known forever
on a cheek I have missed as long:
beautiful woman, veiled & chaperoned,
the moss is settling, the ivy changing colour,
come home, come home ...

Love Poem, My Back to the Fraser

Whale jaw, jack spring spine, rock cod gill,
scallop under the skin of my hand; these
are the bones I'm burying now. Tomcat skull,
sparrow wing, spaniel paw, full moon behind
my bluest gaze; I'm planting them all.
No animal returns to gnaw its gnawed limb
left in a trap; I've thirty years to dig
the deep six for, and hard shoulderblades
to gunnysack. Darling, carry the spade
for me, chant my years without you down;
I want the sunlight on a new foundation,
my old bricks in the wormsweet ground.
Cattle hock, heron claw, muskrat rib,
mast I hang my breathing from; I'll part
the grass and roll the die; I'll build
new castanets: here's a fresh gentility:
as the hummingbird twines its tiny nest
of spiderweb and moss, so I build
my hope and sleep from the marrow
of your kiss.

Two A.M.

For three nights, snow. The gentle steps
of your days disappear, but your body,
at least, is safe, sleeping now beside
me while the city snowploughs
push your lovely journeys to the
curb. I cannot close my eyes
for fear your body is the fallen snow
and nothing in my touch or voice
can keep the night from filling in
the journeys you have granted
to my life. I lie awake and
listen to the awful grind of
scything in the pure fields
of the earth, and cannot bring myself
to understand the snowfall also
means the losing of my heavier path,
the many steps I took unconscious
of your presence in the world,
but then, in the middle of some
placid dream, you run your hand
across my chest, so lightly
I cannot even feel the dark,
red drifts you've pushed beyond
my breathing so I can know
the promise of undreamed avenues,
tomorrow filling in
one flake at a time.

An Evening

The lilacs have bloomed and you go out to pick them
holding the scissors like a small divining rod.
Your bare feet leave impressions in the wet grass
and the cherry tree fills them with blossom.
All day I have been reading Chekhov's stories
and lingering over his paragraphs on love. How sad
his characters are, always meeting too late, then
parting forever before the train leaves the station.
Tears, snowflakes in gaslight, a lowered lorgnette.
And a loveless marriage in the town of S——. I'm sure
there's a story about lilacs I haven't found, and a
beautiful woman cutting perfume from the sky. I'm sure
I can find faded blossoms where her passage graced
the earth. But why should I look? You are standing
in the immaculate motes of an April twilight, bunches
of lilacs blooming from the pale vases of your arms,
and when I lay my book down and walk out to you,
all my bones begin to tremble, divining a straight path
through the musk of evening's beauty and your own,
twin pools my body sinks into beneath a shy, new moon.

Spectrum

In Ireland, I ran up a steep hill to try to prove my youth,
but green defeated me, green laid me down, green wrapped
my body in its Irish embrace, and laid it, breathless,
down.

On the Fraser River, I took the lives of salmon to try to live my own,
but silver defeated me, silver laid me down, silver touched
my body with fleet kisses, and laid it, trembling,
down.

It took your blue eyes to teach me how the colours always win,
and how in their winning is our victory; again and again,
in every way, your blue defeats me, your blue lays me down,
your blue caresses my body, and lays it, as on green grasses,
as in silver schools, rapturously, rapturously,
down.

Speculation on Those Who Have Had Affairs with Famous Poets

The students John Berryman slept with
have graduated into the last third of their lives
now and no longer carry the musk of the poet
to their beds, not even after wine and laughter
or moody evenings alone with the Dream Songs.
The body, after all, is finally just a word
we can't capture in metre; it stops singing
when the blood that gives it meaning stills.

And the mistresses of Earle Birney have blown
their white youth off like dandelion seed
and retire to their shared or solitary sleep
with perhaps a fondness for his memory
but no limb remembering his metrical weight;
there is only a restless phantom of it
in his many lines, the longing of chalk
for the board, the long ride of salt
to the shore. The page under a dead poet's
song is always a little like a bleached sky
of jackdaws on the day of Fame's funeral;
the fire rages, but it can't spread
unless it seeks to burn the greener wood.

The spark in the grain is our philandering tongue.
No one is physical enough in memory to warm a bone.
We all walk out of those rooms where we loved most,
leaving the volume of the moonlight turned down
just a notch, our last trail of footprints from
the shower gone, and maybe a woman falling asleep
over a Collected or the latest quarterly, each
of her pale hands holding the brown monarch
of an age spot so tenderly that it might be
the soul of someone flown, whom she never knew,
except as a dalliance of song
on its lonely flight to posterity.

Reply to William Carlos Williams' "Danse Russe"

Unable to sleep because the word eludes me,
the sweet hieroglyph that wipes blood
from the slate of the self;
unable to sleep because the moon
falls across my body like a corpse
and whispers
"whose death does your love prevent?",
I come to the kitchen table in darkness.

The pen in my hand is claw-cold
and scratches without sense,
without feeling, on a sheet of paper
I can barely see; the wall clock
ticks, a ruthless metronome of thought,
one missed beat, and the rhythm,
the scale of existence is lost.

Suddenly the scent of ripening peaches
fills the room and stays my aimless hand:
I had forgotten them, placed on the windowsill
to quicken with the morning light;
invisible, yet within my reach,
the mind of the fruit thinks "summer,"
thinks "warmth," concentrates its power
until the flesh is soft and full,
until the grasses of dawn
drip a succulent dew.

Unable to sleep: elusive word! elusive life!
All night
I press my hands against my skull
and feel the bruises deepen.

A Small Essay in Honour of the Past

> The soul of a journey is liberty, perfect liberty, to think, feel,
> do just as one pleases. We go a journey chiefly to be free of all
> impediments, and of all inconveniences, to leave ourselves
> behind.
>
> —William Hazlitt

For just one night, to be William Hazlitt
going a journey at the end of the eighteenth century,
deliciously alone on the road to some walled and turretted
town with a Hog's Head Inn and amber lamplight puddling the gloom.
To anticipate steaming viands and whole goblets of tea and a long
repose with a letter carried with me from London. To recite
as I stroll some favourite lines by my good friend, Coleridge,
something about green upland swells and bleating flocks. To own
my mind in a solitude so pure only a bottle of sherry and
a cold chicken could bring me back to the physical world.
Is it too much to want this, for just one night, at the end
of the twentieth century? A few quiet hours on a narrow road
lit by stars? A groom whispering tender praise to my fatigue
as he leads it to the stable? The Irish setter of a fire curled
at my feet, growling at my one foe, worry, in his sleep?
Somewhere the ghost of Hazlitt approaches an old village
at nightfall, delighting in dreams of onion-smothered rabbit.
He refuses to believe his lips are cold and that the Host
of the Hog's Head will not take his useless coins. I love
his obstinance in the face of death. O for just one night,
to be the warm body supping pleasure in his wake.

The Career (1615)

Facing debts with a young bride snatched
from his employer's care, Donne threw over
politics for the pulpit, the blood in fleas
for the caked life in the palms of Christ.
And the crowds amassed to hear him preach
were crushed and fainted in the press.

Master craftsman, dramatist of the flesh
in urgency, he stage-managed his own death,
posing for a painter in his winding-sheet
and saying goodbye to his friends, each
one following the other into the sickroom,
summoned to hear the wisdom of a final speech.
Did he choose the Word or did the Word choose him?
Curious the path of language to the breath of man.

For a Poet Executed at the Gallows

"My youth is gone, and yet I am but young"

—Chidiock Tichborne

Tonight my pen is moving to the pace
of your hung heels, back and forth, back
and forth, that easy, Elizabethan grace
you learned almost at the breast. Chidiock
Tichborne. What a curious and comic name
to meet so ugly a fate. You should have been
a gentleman-courtier to wizened age, bedecked
in gay weeds to sonneteer a privileged place
and pension. Instead, you lived a Catholic
life in a Protestant realm, inevitably faced
charges of conspiracy against the Crown,
composed your one verse in a cell, to whit:
"The fruit is dead, and yet the leaves be green,"
an elegy for yourself, vital, doomed, and young.
Then, one insignificant morning in the year
of your Lord fifteen hundred and eighty six,
you gathered up your ornate name, and swung.

Tonight, alone in my small apartment, I sit
at my writing desk, with four centuries between
us, and my full pint of porter almost run.
I have no faith in your God, am neither Catholic
nor Protestant, and though my country has a Queen
who's English, her influence is nearly gone.
Yet I feel the chill wall of your verse on my back.
Chidiock, my ink is the shade of your swollen tongue
and flows, though I wish I'd kept the pages clean
to record something of the world you loved, sun-
light on your lady's cheek, moon against the black
of Heaven, perhaps a dream of freedom for your faith.
"The spring is past, and yet it hath not sprung."
I would like to face the world with so much grace

that the world would always know my love of it.
But too often now I seem to join the general plague
my century turns upon itself, to feed its young
a glory built on misery and coin, to make us sick
before we feel a sickness in our flesh. Chidiock,
we seem in spirit almost married to the grave.
Like you, our thread is cut before it's spun,
we trod the earth and know it is our tomb, yet
why should a poet swing four hundred years
for us, rooks on his skull, gnats in his grin,
if we can't dance his youthful dance for him?

Faith

The cherries ripen around their pits. The sky
reddens around the sun. My body darkens around
my bones as I stand in the orchard grass and age.
It is all the same, the season and the day and what
the spirit grows toward and loves. I can't remember
if I'm nine or seventeen or thirty-one, but something
in my eye is pit and sun and bone, and the flesh
that ripens around it ripens the rhythm on my tongue.
Ladybug, ladybug, fly away home, your house
is on fire and your children all alone.
The world is a cry in red that calls
the smallest life to care. We cry and care
in the one seared voice, to crack the pit
and the sun and the bone. When spirit loves
its flesh and does not flinch from the burn,
the black ash yields the ripening word.

Acknowledgements

For their encouragement, good humour, and understanding of poetic licence, I wish to thank my parents, Heck & Jean Bowling; my sister, Nola; and my brothers, Rick & Bruce, and their families.

A special thanks to Marisa Alps for all her hard work on my behalf.

My appreciation for their insights and support also goes out to the following: Norm Sacuta, Bert Almon, Russell Thornton, everyone at Harbour Publishing/Nightwood Editions, Don Domanski, Don McKay, John Pass, Stephanie Bolster, Curtis Gillespie, Pat Jasper, Joan Bridgeman and Molly Rychter and the rest of the members of the Hope Writers' Guild, Jacqueline Dumas and the staff at Orlando Books, Don McGrath, Dan "Road Trip" Aire, Charles "Cap" Hutchinson and C. Desmond Blande and all the curmudgeons at *Flash* Magazine, and finally, Homer Pickle (wherever you are!).

In addition, I'd like to thank the editors of the following magazines and anthologies where some of these poems first appeared: *Breathing Fire*, *BC Studies*, *Canadian Author*, *Canadian Forum*, *Clockwatch Review* (U.S.), *Descant*, *Event*, *Fiddlehead*, *Fiddlehead Gold*, *Florida Review* (U.S.), *Georgia Review* (U.S.), *Grain*, *Malahat Review*, *Nimrod* (U.S.), *Poetry Canada*, *Prism*, *Queen's Quarterly*, *Stroll of Poets Anthology*, *Vintage 93*, *Vintage 94*, and *Writers' Forum* (U.K.). I'm grateful as well to the Alberta Foundation for the Arts and to the University of Alberta for financial assistance.